THE Buffalo Jump

written by PETER ROOP

illustrated by BILL FARNSWORTH

rising moon

Books for Young Readers from Northland Publishing

Buffalo Jump was previously published as "Small Deer and the Buffalo Jump" in *Cobblestone Magazine,* and *Little Blaze and the Buffalo Jump* by the Council for Indian Education in cooperation with the Heart Butte School Bilingual Program of the Blackfeet Indian Reservation, Montana.

www.northlandpub.com

The illustrations were rendered in oil on linen
The text type was set in Columbus
The display type was set in Celestia Antique
Composed in the United States of America

Manufactured in Hong Kong

First Impression 1996

03   04   05   7   6   5

ISBN 0-87358-731-6

Library of Congress Catalog Card Number 95-39417
Library of Congress Cataloging-in-Publication Data
Roop, Peter.
The buffalo jump / by Peter Roop ; illustrated by Bill Farnsworth.
p. cm.
Summary: Angry that his older brother is chosen to be the buffalo runner who lures the buffalo to their deaths, Little Blaze, the fastest runner of his Blackfeet tribe, must overcome his resentment when his brother's life is endangered.
ISBN 0-87358-616-6 (hc) ISBN 0-87358-731-6 (sc)
1. Siksika Indians—Juvenile fiction. [1. Siksika Indians—Fiction.
2. Indians of North America—Fiction.] I. Farnsworth, Bill, ill. II. Title.
PZ7.R6723Bu 1996
[Fic]—dc20   95-39417

For Connie, my constant companion.
We've enjoyed buffalo steaks over chip fires under
star-sprinkled skies beneath buffalo jumps. Let's jump
at more of the same! —P. R.

For my wife, Deborah, and my daughters, Allison
and Caitlin. —B. F.

Little Blaze threw back the buffalo robe covering the lodge entrance. He picked up his bow and arrows from where he had thrown them. He knew a brave must always treat his weapons with respect, but now he didn't care. An angry fire flared inside him.

He notched an arrow and aimed at a raven. Little Blaze remembered that *Omuk-may-sto,* the Raven, was good medicine for his people. He would bring bad luck upon his family if he harmed the bird. Still, Little Blaze wanted to strike out against something, anything, to make him feel better.

Little Blaze ducked behind a lodge when he saw Morning Eagle. His friend had seen him disappear and easily discovered Little Blaze.

"Why are you hiding from me?" asked Morning Eagle.

"I don't want to see anyone," growled Little Blaze.

"Even me? Aren't we friends?"

"Yes, you're my friend. But even a friend can do nothing for me."

"Tell me what spirit angers you," said Morning Eagle.

"It is no spirit. It is my father!"

"Your father?" asked Morning Eagle. "What has he done that his son storms around camp like somebody possessed by an evil spirit?"

"He has chosen Curly Bear to be the *ahwa waki,* the buffalo runner. He will stampede the buffalo over the jump tomorrow," Little Blaze said.

"Curly Bear is your brother. He will bring glory to your family."

"But I can run faster than he can," Little Blaze cried, angrily yanking a handful of grass from the earth.

"Doesn't your father know this?"

"He does. He still says that Curly Bear will lead the buffalo over the jump because he is the eldest son. As second son I must stay behind the stacked stones and only help frighten the buffalo."

"Your father has spoken. You must obey him," Morning Eagle said.

"My father is wrong. Curly Bear may be as fast as the antelope, but I am as fast as the wind," Little Blaze said, tossing the grass into the air and watching the wind carry it away. "I should lead the buffalo over the jump. Besides, I am tired of my name. I want to change it like you did. I hate the child's name, Little Blaze."

Morning Eagle looked at his friend. He saw the disappointment in his face. He saw the anger in his heart.

"There is nothing to be done," said Morning Eagle. "You can't change your name until you do something brave. You must forget your anger. Come, let's hunt along the river bottoms for deer. *Omuk-may-sto* brings us his good luck."

"No!" Little Blaze said. "You go."

Little Blaze watched Morning Eagle until he was out of sight. Then he turned and walked in the other direction.

Little Blaze walked fast. Then he began to run, and threw away all thoughts of his brother and the jump

and let his feet carry him where they would. As he ran, Little Blaze felt his anger fading away just as a crackling fire dies out at night.

Little Blaze found himself at the *piskun,* the buffalo jump cliff. He stopped at the edge and looked down. Far below he could see the smoke-white buffalo bones from his tribe's earlier jumps. He kicked a rock over the edge and watched it bounce down the steep slope.

Many times before Little Blaze had seen his people drive a buffalo herd over the cliff. Each jump meant food for his people and new buffalo skins for robes and lodges. A jump was also a chance for the *ahwa waki* to earn a new name. If only his father would let him lead the herd to the cliff!

Little Blaze turned away from the cliff. He walked between the stacks of stones marking the entrance to the jump. The twin rows of stone stacks opened wide like the jaws of a hungry wolf. He knew tomorrow he would be standing behind one of the stone piles, waiting to leap up and frighten the charging buffalo.

Suddenly Little Blaze turned around and began running with all of his might to the edge of the cliff. Little Blaze ran faster and faster. In front of him was the empty air beyond the cliff's edge. In the distance he could see where the earth and sky met once again.

Without stopping Little Blaze ran over the edge of the cliff. The air whizzed by. Then, as he knew he would, Little Blaze landed in a small cup of rock jutting out from the cliff. Many braves had landed on this thin ledge as hundreds of buffalo flashed by to their deaths below.

Little Blaze lay in the cup catching his breath and dreaming he was leading the herd tomorrow. If only he could be the *ahwa waki*. He already knew what new name he would choose.

But it was only a dream. His father had spoken.

As the sun sank behind the Backbone-of-the-World Mountains Little Blaze returned to camp. He hastily ate his dinner and lay down on his buffalo-robe bed.

In the morning Little Blaze joined the other warriors for their daily swim. Then, after a quick breakfast, he followed the men and boys as they walked the trail to the buffalo jump.

Long before the sun rolled into the sky Curly Bear had gone in search of buffalo. No one knew when he would find a herd to drive back. But they must be prepared when he returned with the thundering herd.

Each warrior positioned himself behind one of the stacks of stones. Little Blaze hid with Morning Eagle.

The sun burned down. Little Blaze and Morning Eagle gave up battling the biting flies. The heat made the land dance in the distance. Both boys strained their eyes for the dust of the approaching herd.

Morning Eagle saw the cloud of dust first.

"There, beyond the last pile of rocks," he cried.

Little Blaze squinted until he saw it too. Then, he ran to his father. "They come! We saw their dust," he said.

"*Hyi!* You're right, my son. Your brother leads a good herd. Now quickly get back to your place."

Little Blaze sprinted back. Now he could see Curly Bear running swiftly in front of a small herd of buffalo.

"Ah, we will eat well tonight, Little Blaze," whispered Morning Eagle.

"Yes, it's a good herd," Little Blaze said with only a hint of sadness in his voice. "I only wish it was me out in front."

"Maybe next year your father will choose you," suggested Morning Eagle.

Little Blaze grunted and kept looking at the herd. He
could see Curly Bear very well now. Suddenly he grabbed
Morning Eagle.

"Curly Bear is not very far in front of the herd!"

"*Hyi!* You're right! The buffalo will run him down!"

The stampeding herd was an arrow's shot behind Curly
Bear as he reached the first stack of stones. The braves leapt
into the air, waving skins and shouting. The frightened
buffalo entered the funnel of rocks.

The hard hooves of the buffalo beat the earth like thunder. Curly Bear slowed down just when he needed to be running his very fastest.

Curly Bear passed the third, the fourth, the fifth stone stack. At each one, braves shouted and waved. The buffalo gained on Curly Bear until they were less than a spear's throw behind his tiring feet.

As Curly Bear neared Little Blaze's stack he turned and looked back. He never saw the sharp stone sticking up in front of him. Curly Bear hit the rock running and tumbled into a heap.

Little Blaze dashed to his brother. He grabbed Curly Bear under his arms and yanked him to his feet. The ground rocked with the crash of the buffalo.

Little Blaze ran with Curly Bear to the cliff's edge. The buffalo got closer and closer. Then, like stones dropped into a pond, the two boys disappeared. The stampeding buffalo followed. One by one the herd plunged over the cliff.

In the narrow cup, Little Blaze hugged his older brother. Close to their heads sharp hooves clawed wildly for the suddenly missing ground. The earth shook as the buffalo crashed far below the huddled boys.

Then a strange silence filled the air. Little Blaze looked up. No more buffalo hurtled past them. He lifted Curly Bear to his feet. The boys watched the tribe gather below to butcher the dead buffalo.

Little Blaze heard a voice call from above them.

"Come, my sons. The sun has shone on our tribe. Let us celebrate this good jump. And let us celebrate the brave deeds of both my sons."

That night, after a huge meal of boiled buffalo ribs, Little Blaze was called before his father.

"Little Blaze, today without thinking of your own safety, you ran in front of the buffalo and saved your brother. When any warrior does a deed of courage he is given a new name to honor his act. I give you the name Charging Bull."

Hyi! Charging Bull! Little Blaze could scarcely believe his father's words. Just the name he had wanted for himself. He felt a warm glow spreading through his body like sunshine after a storm.

Charging Bull, a good name. It was a name that would be spoken with pride around Blackfeet campfires for many moons to come.

A Note on the Story

Millions of bison, commonly called buffalo, once roamed America's plains and prairies. Long before horses galloped over the land, Native Americans armed with arrows and spears hunted buffalo on foot. A successful hunt was the key to survival. The great shaggy beasts provided food, shelter, and clothing. A poor hunt meant starvation and death.

Different methods were used to hunt buffalo. Sometimes a lone hunter stalked a small herd on foot, hoping to get close enough to make a kill. Other times large groups, even whole villages, joined together to make a kill big enough to feed the tribe for the winter. *The Buffalo Jump* is based on the prehistoric hunting method of driving a buffalo herd over a cliff.

To decoy a herd the buffalo runner, wearing a wolf or buffalo skin as a disguise, cautiously approached the grazing buffalo. Each herd had a lead animal, usually a cow, which the other buffalo would follow. The buffalo runner attracted the attention of the lead cow. The cow, curious about the "new animal," would come closer to see just what it was. The buffalo runner would then move farther away. If his luck held, the cow would follow, bringing the herd with her. The buffalo runner would then begin to move away more quickly. If the herd continued to follow, the buffalo runner would throw off his robe and break into a run. If his deception worked, the whole herd would stampede behind the sprinting buffalo runner.

Buffalo jumps were best in the fall when a herd was easier to decoy. Disguised under a buffalo or wolf skin, a fast runner stampeded a herd to a cliff where other hunters were waiting. This decoy, the Blackfeet *ahwa waki,* then jumped over the cliff, landed on a ledge, and watched as the buffalo crashed to the ground. Any buffalo not killed in the fall would be shot with arrows or speared by hunters waiting below.

After the buffalo jump, the tribe gathered to skin the animals, cut up the meat, and tend the cooking fires. Every part of the buffalo was used.

The meat was eaten immediately or dried for future use. Skins were tanned and made into sturdy tipis and soft shirts, skirts, and moccasins. Thick wooly buffalo robes kept out winter's chill. Bones were shaped into needles, scrapers, and other tools. Horns became drinking cups and ladles. Rib bones made wonderful sleds. Pouches from bladders were waterproof. Intestines became war charms. Buffalo hair and strips of hide were woven into ropes. Skulls were used in religious ceremonies.

A successful buffalo jump was indeed a joyous occasion.

Buffalo jump sites are scattered throughout the western United States and Canada. The site that inspired this story is the Madison Buffalo Jump in Montana. Standing on the cliff, looking down at the ledge where the *ahwa waki* landed as a thundering herd of buffalo plunged over the cliff, made me wonder what would happen if . . . ?

The answer is *The Buffalo Jump.*

A portion of the profits from this book will be donated toward
the protection and expansion of the bison habitat.

The author would like to thank the Society of Children's Book Writers and
Illustrators for its generous Work-In-Progress grant, which supported research for
The Buffalo Jump. *The Council for Indian Education and the Blackfeet Nation*
are thanked, too, for first publishing Little Blaze and the Buffalo Jump *so that*
Native American children could learn about their ancestors. Thanks to Cobblestone
Magazine *for also publishing the story.*

The illustrator offers special thanks to Steve DiPietro and Marlin Spoonhunter.

About the Author and Illustrator

CONNIE B. ROOP

PETER ROOP received his Master's in Children's Literature in 1980 from the Center for the Study of Children's Literature at Simmons College in Boston, and has since published more than twenty children's books. Seven of these, including *Keep the Lights Burning, Abbie,* are co-authored with his wife, Connie, and are Reading Rainbow Books. Peter has written many articles and stories about Native Americans for *Cobblestone Magazine,* where *The Buffalo Jump* was published in an earlier form. His stories have also appeared in *Cricket, Jack and Jill, Highlights,* and *Short Story International.* His first three children's books were about the Blackfeet Indians and were all published by the Council for Indian Education.

The 1986 Wisconsin State Teacher of the Year, Peter currently teaches grades one and two. Peter and Connie live in Appleton, Wisconsin, with their two children, Sterling, fourteen, and Heidi, eleven.

STEVE DiPIETRO

BILL FARNSWORTH, a graduate of the Ringling School of Art and Design in Sarasota, Florida, and member of the Society of Illustrators and The Air Force Art Program, provides illustrations for such clients as *Tennis Magazine* and *Reader's Digest,* Harcourt Brace & Co., Bantam Doubleday Dell, and Simon & Schuster.

As research for the illustrations in *The Buffalo Jump,* Bill traveled to Browning, Montana, the heart of the Blackfeet Reservation, and photographed Blackfeet models, buffalo, and the original buffalo jump sites. He also visited the Plains Indians Museum in Browning, the Head Smashed-In Buffalo Jump Interpretive Center in Alberta, Canada, and the Museum of Natural History.

Bill lives in Venice, Florida, with his wife, Deborah, and daughters Allison and Caitlin.